Just Like My Papa

by Toni Buzzeo

Illustrated by Mike Wohnoutka

DISNEY • HYPERION BOOKS

NEW YORK

First Edition
10 9 8 7 6 5 4 3 2 1
F850-6835-5-13001
Printed in Singapore
Designed by Michelle Gengaro-Kokmen

Library of Congress Cataloging-in-Publication Data

Buzzeo, Toni.
Just like my Papa / Toni Buzzeo ; illustrations by Mike Wohnoutka.—1st ed.
p. cm.
Summary: A lion cub wants to emulate his father, the king of the pride.
ISBN 978-1-4231-4263-8 (hardcover)
[1. Lion—Fiction. 2. Animals—Infancy—Fiction. 3. Fathers and sons—Fiction.] I. Wohnoutka, Mike, ill. II. Title.
PZ7.B9832Ju 2013
[E]—dc23   2011011153

Visit www.disneyhyperionbooks.com

With love and gratitude to John Mackey,
who has been in my corner from the very beginning
—T.B.

To Olivia and Franklin, from their Papa
—M.W.

ROAAAAAR!

A warning echoes across the plain.
Yellow moon peeks over the horizon.

Kito peeks too.
His papa paces and roars again:
*My pride is here. Stay away!
I am the protector and King.*

The savanna falls silent.

grooooowl!

Kito adds his warning:

I am here too.
Just like my papa, the King.

Hyena laughs and creeps nearby.
Kito drops down in the tall grass and shivers.

Yellow moon slides into sleep.
Kito slides into sleep too
while Papa keeps watch.

When sun burns hot in the sky,
Papa sprawls in the shade of the
acacia tree.
Flies buzz around him.
He swings his long tail.
The tuft of handsome hair
sweeps flies away on the wind.
Stay away!
I am the protector and King.

Kito swings his little golden tail.
I will keep you away too.
Just like my papa, the King.
But the flies keep *buzz*
buzz
buzzing.

Kito prances near to Papa.
He pounces on Papa's back.

Wheeeeeeeeee!

With a swipe of his huge paw,
Papa sends Kito flying through the air,
like a stork gliding on the breeze.

Thump!

Kito lands on his rump,
then rushes back to Papa.
Again?

Wheeeeeeeeee!

Thump!

Wheeeeeeeeee!

Thump!

Papa growls,
Enough, Little Kito.
I am busy being King.

Kito lies in the tall grass.
I am busy too.
Just like my papa, the King.

When sun slips toward blue twilight,
Papa stands and gives his dark brown
mane a fearsome shake.
He follows the lionesses to the hunt.

Kito shakes his little head.
He sneaks off after Papa.
I will hunt too.
Just like my papa, the King.

The pride follows the wildebeest herd.
They watch carefully for the slowest wildebeest.

Suddenly the lionesses run.
The wildebeest runs too.
Papa's powerful legs and strong jaws
wait for the moment of capture.

Kito waits too, at the edge of the brush.
He flexes his small legs.
He snaps his little jaws at the flies nearby.
Buzz buzz buzz.
Snap snap snap!

The slowest wildebeest
is one minute faster than the lionesses.
The wildebeest escapes.
But—*snap!*
Hungry Kito catches his fly.

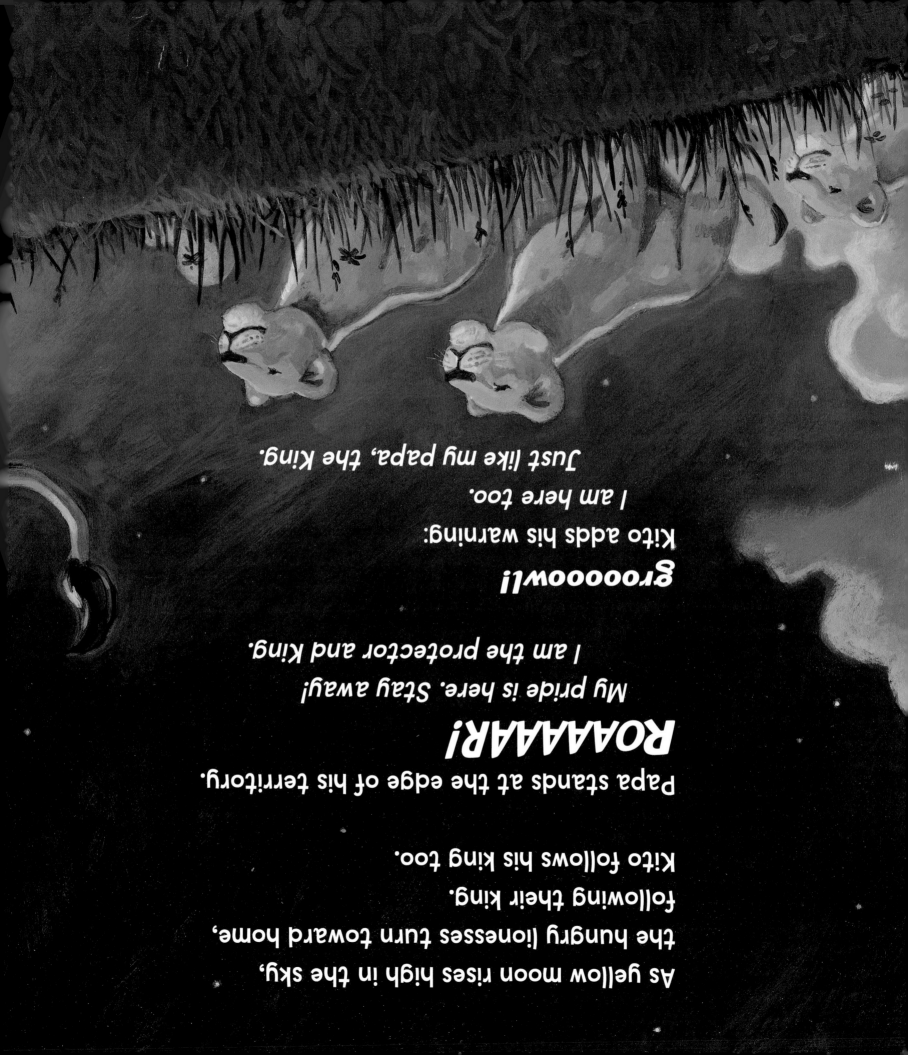

As yellow moon rises high in the sky,
the hungry lionesses turn toward home,
following their king.
Kito follows his king too.

Papa stands at the edge of his territory.

ROAAAAR!

My pride is here. Stay away!
I am the protector and King.

grooooowl!

Kito adds his warning:
I am here too.
Just like my papa, the King.

Papa settles down in golden moonlight.
Come here, my brave little hunter.
Help me to be King.

Kito climbs onto Papa's back.
He waves his little tail.
He shakes his little head.
He rakes his paw gently through his papa's mane.
He growls softly.

I am here.

Someday I will be King.

Just like my papa.

Author's Note

In Swahili, the name *Kito* means "precious gem." A pride of lions consists of five or six lionesses, a male lion (or occasionally two), and their cubs. Through play, lion cubs practice skills they'll need for hunting when they are older. The job of the male of the pride is to keep invaders out of their territory by patrolling and roaring. For most of the day, the lions rest together in the shade, often for as long as twenty hours, but when dusk comes, it is time for hunting. It is often the female lions who stalk and kill the prey, but after the prey is killed, the male lion is the first to feast.